"See that you don't look down on one of these little ones. Here is what I tell you. Their angels in heaven can go at any time to see my Father who is in heaven."

Matthew 18:10-11

Angels, Angels Everywhere

WRITTEN BY
Larry Libby

ILLUSTRATED BY
Corbert Gauthier

Zonderkidz

Angels, Angels Everywhere
ISBN: 0-310-70342-5
Copyright © 2003 by Larry Libby
Illustrations © copyright 2003 by Corbert Gauthier

Requests for information should be addressed to:

Zonder**kidz** ®

The children's group of Zondervan

Grand Rapids, Michigan 49530

Previously published by Gold-n-Honey

Zonderkidz is a trademark of Zondervan.

Editor: Gwen Ellis
Art Direction: Laura Maitner

Printed in China
03 04 05 /HK/ 4 3 2 1

For Dad and Mom …
who showed me the way.

Larry Libby

———————————————

To parents everywhere, who take the
time to read with their children.

Corbert Gauthier

Do Angels Know Where We Are?

id you know God's angels are with you no matter where you are—on a mountaintop, in a valley, or even in a desert. An angel found the prophet Elijah in the middle of the desert. Elijah had gone there to escape the evil King Ahab and Queen Jezebel. He thought he was alone when he curled up to go to sleep. But he wasn't.

The Bible says: "Suddenly an angel touched him. The angel said, 'Get up and eat'" (1 Kings 19:5).

Elijah must have been surprised. It's not every day an angel wakes you from your nap. And what was that delicious smell? He opened his eyes and saw right there in the desert, a flat cake of freshly baked bread to eat and a jug of clear, cool water to drink!

You see, Elijah belonged to God, and God takes care of those who belong to him. God sent his messenger—his angel—to help and encourage Elijah. The angel knew right where Elijah was. And God and his angels know exactly where you are too!

Why Can't We See Angels?

A long time ago, a prophet of God and his servant saw enemy soldiers surrounding the city where they were staying. The servant was afraid, but the prophet was not! He could see something wonderful with his spiritual eyes. The prophet asked God to open his servant's eyes too. Then they both could see an army of angels and fiery chariots and horses protecting them.

There once was a little boy from the city who was afraid to stay overnight at his grandparents' house. They lived in the country. During the day, he played in the creek and explored the woods. But at night it seemed so dark without the city lights. He was so frightened that he would hide his head under his quilts.

The little boy wouldn't have been afraid if he could have seen God's loving angels all around him. If God opened your spiritual eyes, you would see angels sitting on your bed watching over you and standing by your front door to keep you safe.

What Do Angels Look Like?

First of all, the word "angel" means "messenger". They are sent by God to tell people what God wants them to know. Then, the Bible tells us only a little about how angels look. The prophet Isaiah saw angels with six wings. Daniel, another prophet, said: "I looked up and saw a man who was dressed in linen clothes. A belt that was made out of the finest gold was around his waist. His body gleamed like chrysolite (a kind of yellow-green stone). His face shone like lightning. His eyes were like flaming torches. His arms and legs were as bright as polished bronze. And his voice was like the sound of a large crowd" (Daniel 10:5–6).

Wow! Daniel had seen an amazing heavenly being! But sometimes angels look like regular people. Abraham once saw three men coming toward him. He ran to offer them water to wash their feet, bread to eat, and a place to rest. Later, Abraham realized he had been visited by God and two of his angels.

Whether an angel looks like a heavenly being or a regular person, there's one thing we know for sure: angels are God's messengers.

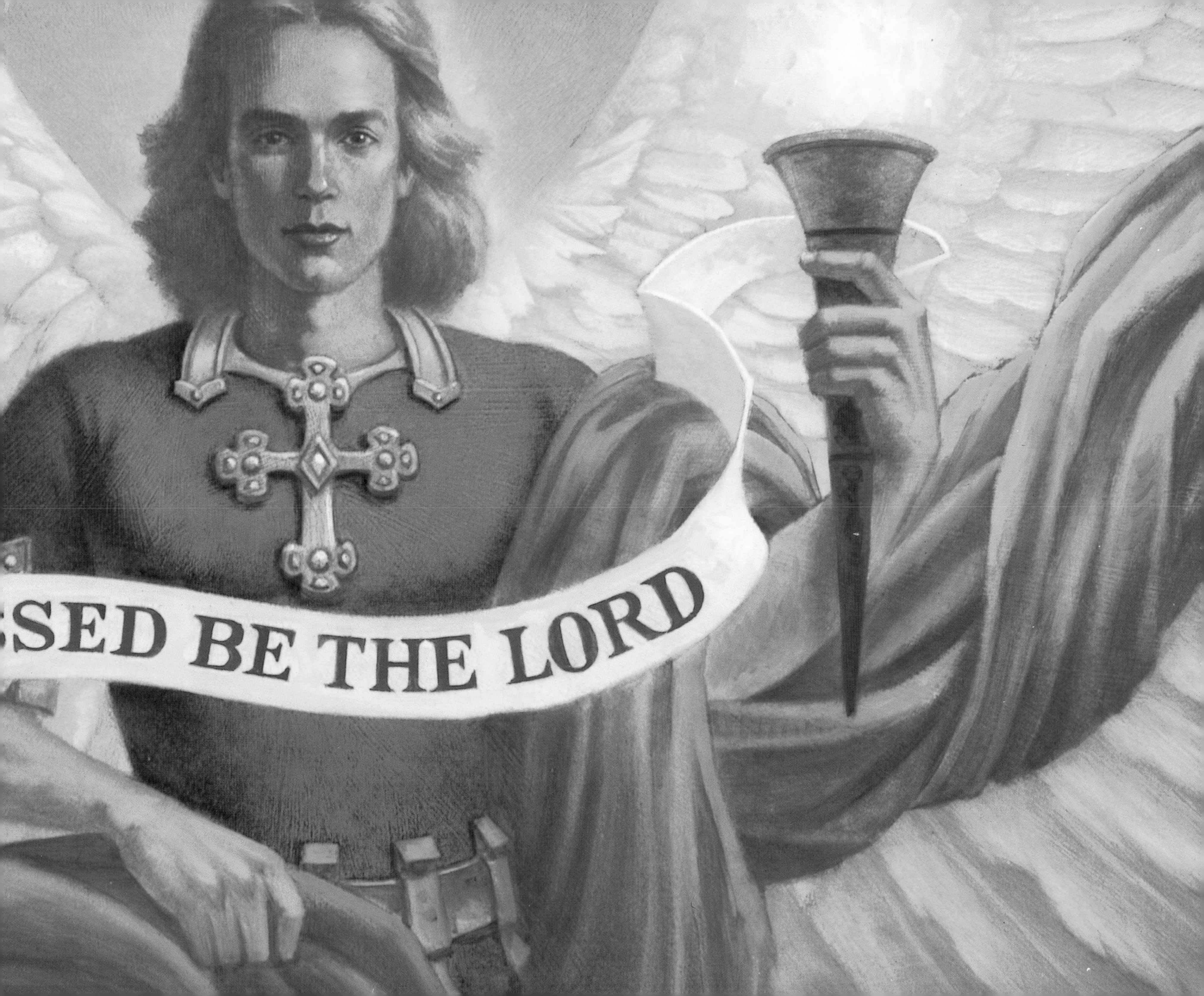
SSED BE THE LORD

Will I Be an Angel When I Die?

No, you couldn't be an angel, even if you were the kindest, best-hearted person who ever lived. Do you know why? Because God made angels, and as far as we know, they have always lived in heaven. He also made people, and we have always lived on earth. Angels and humans are very different. Someday, we humans will leave our old home on earth and move into a sparkling new home in heaven. It will be more beautiful than we can imagine—even in our dreams!

Angels have made-for-heaven bodies, and we have made-for-earth bodies. But when we leave our old earth bodies behind, we will step into new, made-for-heaven bodies. Better bodies. But even then we will not be like the angels. We will be ourselves—just like God created us.

How Do Angels Get to Earth from Heaven?

Some people think angels come and go to heaven on a golden staircase. That's because Jacob once had a dream. "In a dream Jacob saw a stairway standing on the earth. Its top reached to heaven. The angels of God were going up and coming down on it" (Genesis 28:12). Even though those angels used stairs, they don't have to have a staircase to come to earth. They can just come and go whenever God sends them to take care of us.

After Jacob had his dream, he felt as though he had been at the front door of heaven, so he named the place where he had slept "Bethel." That means "the house of God." Did you know that wherever you stop to pray—at the table, in church, beside your bed, or even outside as you watch the shapes of clouds and think about your heavenly Father—that's heaven's front door. And God the Father and his angels are always nearby.

Do Angels Deliver Messages?

Angels are like mail carriers. They deliver messages of hope and love from God to his people.

Once God's angels delivered a special message to a missionary named Paul. He was a prisoner of the Romans. The Romans were taking him across the sea on a ship. Suddenly, the sky began to boil with clouds and rain. The wind howled loudly. The men were afraid. They thought they were going to die.

Then Paul had a visit from a "messenger" angel. The next morning, Paul said, "I belong to God and serve him. Last night his angel stood beside me. The angel said, 'Do not be afraid, Paul … God has shown his grace by sparing the lives of all those sailing with you'" (Acts 27:23–24).

The angel found Paul on the ship, in the middle of the night, in the middle of the sea, in the middle of a storm! When God sends a message of hope and help to his people, his angels will see that it gets delivered.

Do You and I Have a Special Angel?

Jesus once said, "See that you don't look down on one of these little ones. Here is what I tell you. Their angels in heaven can go at any time to see my Father who is in heaven" (Matthew 18:10-11).

Jesus' words tell us that he cares very much about each and every girl and boy. And he sends his angels to protect and watch over them—that includes you. What happy news!

But what does that mean exactly? Does it mean you will never fall off your bicycle or get a cut on your finger? Does it mean that other children won't ever call you names or hurt your feelings? The answer is no. There will still be hurts. But no matter what happens to you, you can be sure that God's angels are right there with you, helping you, and looking after you. You are never alone!

Where Are Angels When We Need Them?

Angels are heaven's secret service agents. It's good to have them nearby. In the Bible, we read about the prophet Daniel. Some evil men tricked the king of Persia into throwing Daniel into a pit of hungry lions. Early the next morning, the worried king came to the edge of the pit and called out to Daniel: "Has God been able to save you?" The king was thrilled to hear Daniel's strong, calm voice from the bottom of the pit. "My God sent his angel. And his angel shut the mouths of the lions. They haven't hurt me at all" (Daniel 6:22).

What caused those lions to change their minds about eating Daniel? An angel shut their mouths! Maybe the lions saw the angel and decided it might be best to leave Daniel alone. Daniel saw the angel too. And he knew God had sent it to save his life.

Angels save the lives of God's people all over the world. They are the strongest friends we can have.

Did Jesus Have Guardian Angels?

Angels watched over Jesus while he lived on earth. When he needed their help, they were always there—like the night before he died on the cross for our sins.

Jesus and his friends had climbed a nearby hillside to pray. He prayed, "Father, if you are willing, take this cup of suffering away from me. But do what you want, not what I want" (Luke 22:42). Then an angel from heaven came to Jesus and gave him strength.

Jesus' friends were asleep when the angel showed up. Jesus was feeling sad and lonely. We don't know exactly how the angel helped Jesus. Maybe the angel wanted to take away his sorrow. Maybe the angel knelt down beside Jesus and whispered a message of love from God, his Father. Maybe the angel reminded Jesus that only he, God's beloved Son, could save us—not one angel or even all the angels in heaven could do it!

Or maybe the angel just scooted up close to Jesus and said, "We all love you, and we can't wait for you to come home."

What Is the Good News Angels Hear in Heaven?

Jesus said, "There will be great joy when one sinner turns away from sin" (Luke 15:7). Just think about that. When even one person on earth—one man, woman, boy, or girl—asks Jesus Christ to be Savior and Lord, it's Big News in heaven.

Jesus said that this makes our heavenly Father as happy as a shepherd who finds his lost, wandering sheep or a woman who finds a lost silver coin or a father who finds a dearly-loved son who has been lost.

The angels are happy too because they know that when we say yes, we are also saying:

YES, I want God to forgive all the bad things in my heart.

YES, I believe that Jesus died on the cross for me.

YES, I believe that Jesus rose from the dead and now lives forever in heaven.

YES, I give all of myself to Jesus Christ.

News of your yes to Jesus flies across heaven before you can blink an eye. It's like a burst of golden fireworks shining on everyone in heaven all at once. And that Big News gives the angels a new song to sing.

Can We Praise God with the Angels?

We know angels sing and praise God all the time. Here is song from the Bible about angels:

Praise the Lord, you angels of his.
Praise him, you mighty ones
who carry out his orders and obey his word.
Praise the Lord, all you angels in heaven.
Praise him, all you who serve him
and do what he wants.
(Psalm 103:20-21)

Think of the best praise song to the Lord Jesus that you know. Sing it with all your heart. The angels will more than likely join in with us as we praise the Lord. They will be singing praises to God even though you might not hear them.

Who knows, your little praise chorus might get something really big started as more and more angels join in. Perhaps by the time you've snuggled down in your bed for the night and closed your eyes, all of heaven might be singing the song that you started in your room!

Do Angels Worship God?

Angels have probably been worshiping God from the moment they first opened their eyes and saw God smile—singing his praises with all their hearts since before there was even an earth or people on it. There are even now special angels around God's throne who never, ever stop praising his name. Singing praise to the Lord is all they want to do, forever and ever.

Once God was talking to a man named Job. God told Job that when he first rolled the Earth into a ball and made it into a world: "The morning stars sang together. All of the angels shouted with joy" (Job 38:7).

What do you think those angels shouted when God sent the beautiful new world spinning like a bright blue marble into space? Maybe they said:

"Oh! It's so beautiful!"

"God, you are so awesome!"

"We praise your name forever!"

We love to praise God right here on earth. And someday, when we get to heaven, we'll be able to praise God and the Lord Jesus right along with the angels. They probably have songs to teach us, and who knows, maybe we can teach them some songs too. Won't that be fun!

What Can We Learn from the Angels?

Angels have seen God's face and know so much about him. The most important thing we can learn from angels is to obey. When God speaks, angels do whatever he asks them to do! They don't take time to think about it, ask questions and argue, look at their watches, or get a drink of water. They just obey. The longer we put off doing what we know is right, the heavier our hearts will feel. That's the most amazing lesson the angels can teach us. Let's be like the angels—quick to obey.

The Bible says
some amazing things
about angels:

Angels are from heaven.
Genesis 28:12

Angels are strong.
2 Thessalonians 1:7

Angels are smart.
Revelation 22:6

Angels are beautiful and good.
Daniel 10:5-9

Angels are joyful.
Job 38:7

Angels can fly and walk through walls
and even step into people's dreams.
Matthew 1:20

Angels are older than the earth.
Job 38:7

Angels watched the creation of our whole universe.
Job 38:4-7

Angels visit our planet all the time.
Acts 12:11

Angels can speak our language.
Luke 1:19

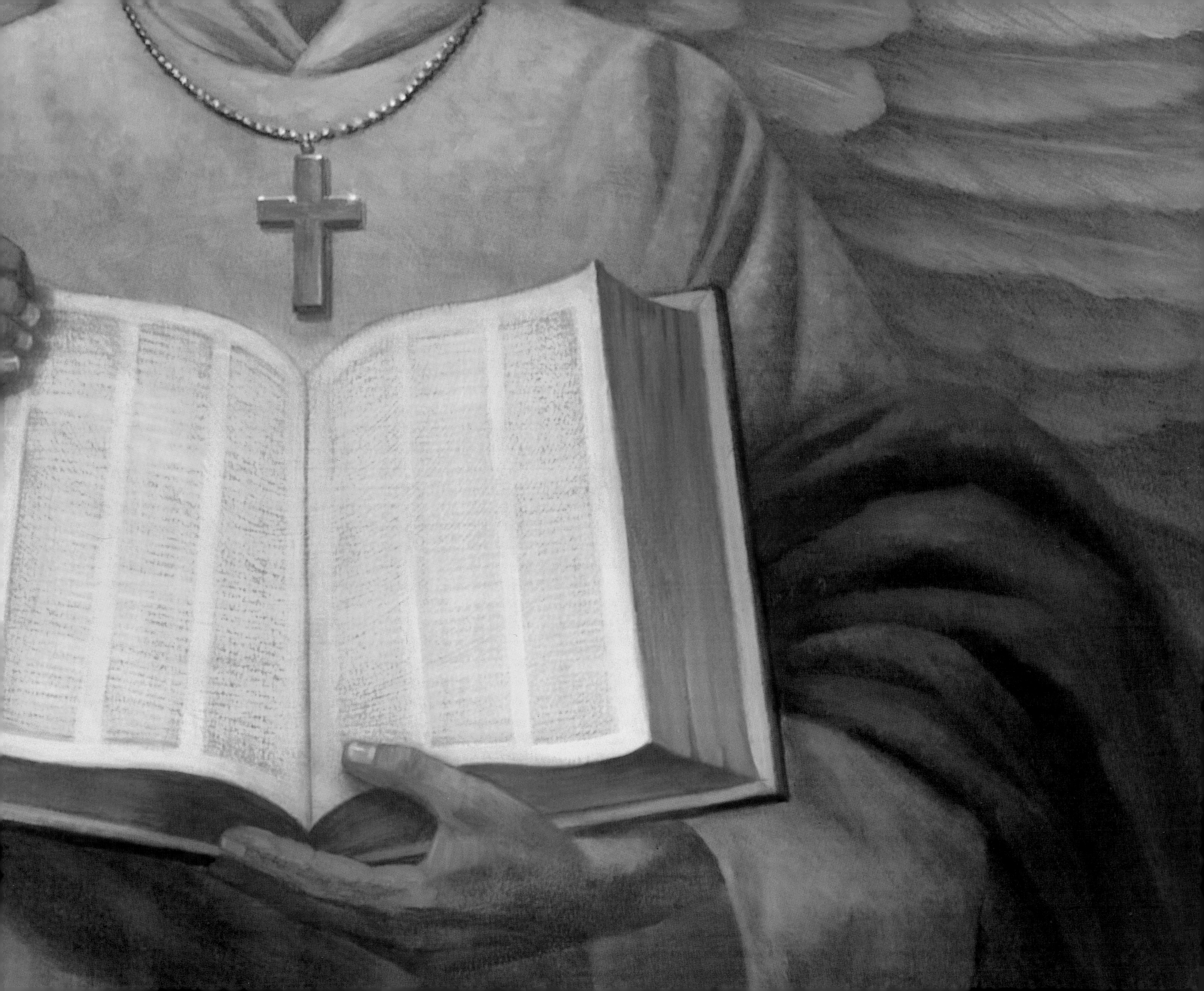

Will Angels Take Me to Heaven?

Jesus once told a story about a man named Lazarus. He was a man who loved God but was very poor, lonely, and sick. When Lazarus died, Jesus said that angels tenderly carried him to heaven where he would never be poor or lonely or sick again.

That sounds like something our heavenly Father would do—send an angel to bring us home because he loves us so much. Every time an angel brings a boy or girl or man or woman to heaven, it's a time of great joy.

When you come to your forever home for the very first time, you will be so happy! You will say, "Oh, my! This is more beautiful than anything I could have dreamed! Is this really my new home?" The angels will be so happy to tell you that it is!

So remember, when it's time to leave earth for heaven, God's angels will meet you and bring you home. But also remember that no matter where you are—here on earth or in heaven above—God's angels are always with you!